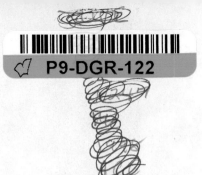
Melody's Incredible Adventure

by
Barbara Neal

Illustrations by
Rebecca Carroll

Independent Books
San Francisco, California

Published by
San Francisco Independent
1201 Evans Avenue
San Francisco, California 94124

Edited by Zoran Basich and Bill Picture
Illustrations by Rebecca Carroll
Book design by Jane Musser

Library of Congress Catalog Number 97-94656
Neal, Barbara
Melody's Incredible Adventure
ISBN 0-9665020-2-7
97-94656

AN INDEPENDENT BOOK

"If we win here we will win everywhere.
The world is a fine place and worth fighting for."
— Ernest Hemingway

Dedicated to my friend, Barbara Fenech
and to the kids at Free Spirit
who encouraged me to write this book.

Prologue

I had just finished revising an article on runaway teens when my editor called me into his office.

"How's the story coming?"

I smiled. "It's almost done."

He nodded and gestured to a chair. "Sit down, Melody." He had that serious look on his face, which usually meant that he was going to tell me something I didn't want to hear. "We want to run an article on the homeless - how they're surviving, what they're feeling, and what hopes they have for the future."

I leaned back in my chair.

"This is a difficult time of the year for most of them," I said. "Time is running out for a lot of them."

He nodded. "We're after news," he said, "and the homeless are news right now. I know how sympathetic you are to them. Maybe I should give this assignment to someone who isn't so involved."

I thought for a moment. I had never turned my back on any story.

If there were something to say, I would say it. "I'll take the assignment," I said.

He smiled. "I had a feeling you would."

Back in my office, I kept thinking about what he said. He was right - the homeless are news. And during this time of year there was lots of publicity about them. One thought kept running through my mind. What could I write that hadn't been written before?

I went to the window and stared out onto the San Francisco street. My gaze was drawn to a boy slowly walking across the street. I continued to watch as he stopped, looked around, then curled up in a doorway, pulling a blanket over his head. Just another homeless kid, I thought. Like hundreds of others in this city. Then the boy raised his head and his eyes seemed to lock with mine. I started thinking about the way his life must affect his family - if he had one. And how anyone living in the streets affects everyone. But the mystery is why some people understand them and others don't want to.

"Well," I thought, "I better get to work."

Until that moment, I wasn't sure how I would write this story. Then I began.

1

Where Has the Spirit Gone?

I can't stop thinking about what happened that Christmas. When I least expect it, I suddenly find myself drifting back into my past. Memories begin to flood my mind and suddenly I'm thirteen again and I relive the pain of my loss.

I thought these memories would fade in time but they hadn't. They seem only to have gotten more detailed over the years. I can still see the Christmas tree blazing away, and how well I remember that I didn't want Christmas to come.

Tears welled up in my eyes. There was only one thing I wanted. I lay on the floor staring at the fire crackling in the fireplace. I brushed away a tear and wondered how many other people had also lost the spirit of Christmas. I remembered Mom always telling me how lucky I was, that there were lots of kids who had no hope, poor kids who were hungry, cold, and homeless. Maybe I should have but I didn't care about those kids. It's not my fault the world is unfair, full of poverty. Anyway, my own life was messed up. I lay there, thinking back. How I wished I could wash away the images of that day.

But they were permanent, and would always be with me. I saw them clearly, the storm, the wind screaming and howling, the thunder and lightning flashing in the sky. I could see her face as clear to me as if I was seeing my own face in a mirror.

I stood at the window and looked out. It wasn't just raining it was coming down in torrents.

"I have to go out for a while," Mom said.

I turned around and looked at her. "It's really coming down."

She glanced out the window, then back at me. "I have to cover this story about some homeless kids living under the freeway."

"Can't it wait?" I asked.

She shook her head. "The police found out they're living there. If I don't see them today, I might not get a chance to talk to them."

I listened to the wind getting louder. "At least wait until the storm lets up."

She put on her coat. "No chance of that. This storm is going to be around for a while."

"I'll come with you," I said.

She looked at me questioningly. "Don't you have homework to do?"

"I did it before," I said quickly. "Honest."

She looked at me dubiously, but she must have believed me for she said, "I'd really like to, kid, but not this time."

"Aw, Mom," I said disappointedly.

She put her hand on my shoulder. "I'm sorry, Melody, but these kids are different. They may not like you being with me. Do you understand?"

I smiled at her. "Sure, Mom, I understand. Next time will be okay."

She gave me a little hug. "Next time," she said and went out.

I smiled at her through the window. She raised her hand and waved to me. Then she got into her car and drove off. I stared after it until it disappeared from my sight.

Hours later I stood at the window staring out into the dark; it was still raining. I was worried. Mom always called when she was going to be late.

As soon as I saw the police car drive up in front of the house, I knew something was wrong. I silently watched the two policemen get out of their car and come to the front door. A few moments later I watched them drive away.

When Dad came into the room I turned to look at him. I felt fear take control of my body.

"Melody," he began, then faltered. He hesitated for a second, then tried again. "Melody ... there's been an accident ... the rain ... her car skidded ... went off the road ...." I stared at him for a moment without seeing him. What was he saying? He moved

closer to me. "Mom is gone," he said, his face suddenly going pale. "She's gone."

I backed away from him. "It's not true," I cried. "It's not true."

I ran for my bedroom and locked myself in. I threw myself across the bed and buried my face into the pillow. I couldn't cry. My eyes were burning but I couldn't cry.

It was morningwhen I opened the door. I saw Dad sitting on the floor, leaning his head against the wall. Seeing the sadness in his eyes, I knew it was true. Mom was really gone. I never felt so much pain before. I wanted Dad to comfort me, to tell me it was all right, even though I knew it wasn't and would never be again. I flung myself into his arms with a sob. "We have to be strong," he said softly. "Your mother would want us to be strong for her."

"It's not fair," I cried, as he held me tightly to him.

"I know," he said. "I know."

My mind drifted back from my memories, back to my surroundings. Slowly I turned to gaze around the room when suddenly I stopped. My eyes rested on the wall over the fireplace where a portrait of my mother hung. "Why did you leave me?" I said angrily, "It hurts too much."

I stared at her picture for several moments. She returned my gaze smiling that familiar smile.

I turned away to eye the tree. Dad wouldn't listen when I told him it was too soon. That we shouldn't celebrate Christmas at all.

"There will be no discussion," he said. "If you don't want to celebrate Christmas, that's fine. But we will have a tree to cele-

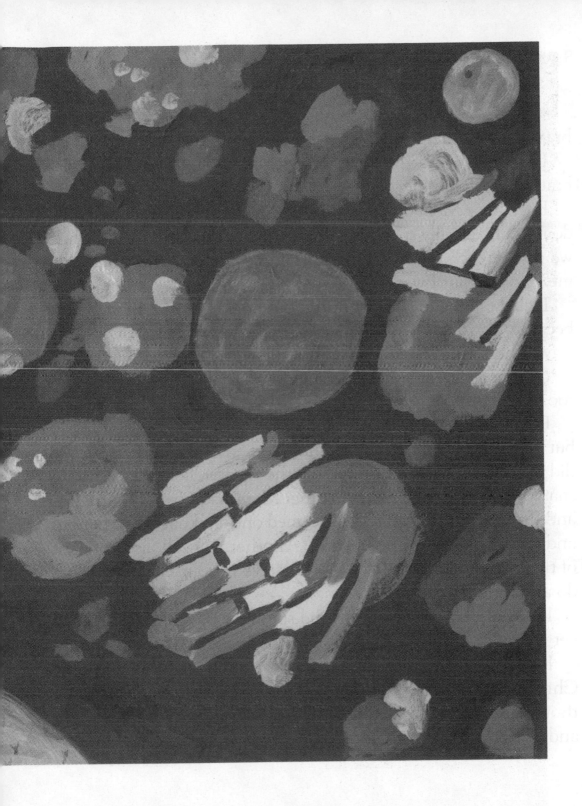

brate your mother's life."

I thought he was losing it. How could a dumb tree be a celebration of Mom's life?

Ever since Mom died, we have grown farther apart. Dad is seldom home, usually spending all his time at the office. And when we do see each other, all we do is argue. He doesn't understand me or care what I want.

I tried talking to Mrs. Connors, our housekeeper. She said that because Christmas was Mom's favorite holiday, the tree was Dad's way of honoring her memory. And she added that I should learn to be more patient and understanding because he misses Mom too.

For me, I knew the pain would never go away. I loved my Dad, but Mom and I had been closer, like we were the same person. We did everything together: shopping, the theater, concerts. And we shared the same interest in writing. Mom had been a journalist, and I wanted to be one, too. I dreamed one day that I'd be famous and write about the whole world. Another tear fell, as I thought of the many times Mom told me, "Believe in yourself and you can do anything."

I missed her so much. Why did she have to die? I didn't even get a chance to say goodbye.

I stared at the glowing lights on the tree. What a lousy Christmas this was going to be. It'll never be the same again, I thought sadly, as I remembered last Christmas Eve. Dad, Mom and I singing Christmas carols while decorating the tree. Dad lifting me to his shoulders to put Mom's angel on top of the tree.

We called it Mom's angel because it had been in her family for generations, passed from daughter to daughter upon marriage.

"Suppose I don't want to get married," I asked her.

She shook her head and laughed merrily. "It doesn't matter," she said. "But if you do, I'll dance at your wedding like this."

Then she took my hands and danced with me up and down the hall, through the living room, and around the Christmas tree.

Later we took gifts to the homeless shelter, a tradition we did every Christmas Eve, for as long as I could remember.

I eyed the tree. Mom's angel was missing.

Dad and Mrs. Connors had searched in all the usual and not-so-usual places where the angel might be. But it was nowhere to be found.

Dad looked perplexed. "Where can it be?"

Mrs. Connors shook her head. "I just can't understand it. I've looked everywhere."

"Obviously not," I mumbled, choosing to ignore both of them as I put on my headphones to listen to some great music.

"Melody, do you know where Mom's angel is?" Dad asked me. I didn't hear him. My head was bobbing in tune to the music.

"Melody," Dad said again, taking off my headphones.

I glared at him. "What?"

He stared at me. "Can't you find more constructive things to do with your time?"

"What's your problem?" I asked.

"I would appreciate a little help from you."

"Give me a break, Dad. What are you talking about?"

"I asked you, do you know where Mom's angel is?"

I shrugged. "How would I know?"

Dad and Mrs. Connors exchanged glances. "Are you sure," she asked, "that you don't know where it is?"

I looked at her coldly. "Nope. I have no idea," I said, instantly defiant.

"Don't be disrespectful," warned my father. "If you don't straighten up, you'll be grounded."

"Oh you mean I'll get to spend more time by myself," I said sarcastically.

He looked at me. There was an intent expression on his face. "We're just trying to figure out what happened to it."

I could see this conversation was going nowhere. "I said I don't know where it is," I said, leaving the room. "Why don't you ever listen to me?"

I'm sick of always being blamed for something I didn't do. Why would I take Mom's angel? That's the dumbest thing I ever heard.

The persistent ringing of the telephone jarred my attention away from my thoughts. Mrs. Connors had gone home, and Dad, as usual, had gone back to his office. If he didn't want to be around me ... well, I didn't care. I didn't need him anyway.

It took me a moment to compose myself, to stop the tears. Then I picked up the phone. I was glad to hear the voice at the other end. It was my best friend Lelani, who has the uncanny ability to sense what I am feeling.

"Hey girl, what's up?"

"Nothing."

"Are you okay?"

"I'm fine."

She paused for a moment, then said, "I'm going shopping tomorrow. Come with me."

"Shopping with you?" I said. "I don't think so."

"Melody, you know I hate shopping alone."

"That's your problem."

I had to hand it to her. She was persistent.

"Come on, Melody, it'll be fun."

"Yeah, for you."

"Macy's has these fantastic hand-knit sweaters that I would absolutely die for," she said, giving a high pitched giggle.

I seldom felt like laughing anymore, but I did this time. Although we didn't always agree on everything, and she could be weird at times ... still, she always knew how to raise my spirits.

As I knew she would, she finally wore down my resistance. I let out a long sigh. "Okay," I said. "I know I'm going to regret this."

"Cool," she said. "I'll see you at the bus stop at ten."

"See you," I said, hanging up the phone.

More than anything, I hated shopping with her. Put Lelani in a department store, and she went crazy, buying things she would never use or wear. But we've been best friends our whole lives. I never could have gotten through those awful days without her. Lelani was the only one who knew how I felt, helping me through my anger and hurt. She was one of a kind. I was glad to have her as a friend.

I was feeling very tired. I had better get to bed if I was going to meet her tomorrow. Shopping with Lelani was bound to be an experience. An overwhelming feeling of sadness came over me as I looked at the tree once more before going upstairs. I realized that even with all of its glitter and ornaments, it was missing the most beautiful ornament of all.

I sighed. Nothing in my life was going right these days. Mom's angel couldn't just disappear.

As I lay in bed, gazing out the window at the stars, I felt drained, no more tears, nothing left but bitterness and acceptance.

The door opened. Dad stuck his head in.

"Hi, Dad."

"I didn't think you'd still be awake," he said, coming in and sitting on the bed.

"I've been thinking, Dad, do you believe in angels?"

He paused. "I'm not sure. I mean, I've never seen one, but there are people who claim they have."

"Mrs. Connors said that because Mom cared about other people, the minute she died she was an angel."

He smiled. "I think she may be right."

"Mom always said everyone had a guardian angel to watch over them and protect them."

He nodded. "Yes, she believed that."

"Dad, why did God let mom die?" I asked.

He was silent for a moment. "I wish I could answer that but sometimes, things happen that we don't understand."

"It's not fair," I said.

"Yeah, well, life isn't always fair," he said wearily.

I studied his face for a moment, then looked away. "Mom used to say you don't always have to see something to know it exists?"

"I remember."

"If there are angels, maybe it would make Mom being gone a little easier to accept."

"Everything will be all right, Melody. You'll be all right."

I looked back at him. "Dad, I can't stop thinking about Mom. How can she be gone if she is still so alive in my memory?"

"Mom will never really be gone. She'll always live in our hearts."

I snuggled down deeper into the cover. After a moment, I said, "I'm not sure I have a guardian angel. I'd like to believe I do."

Dad smiled at me. "Maybe you do."

I'd have to think some more about that.

"Goodnight, honey," he said, kissing me on the forehead.

"Dad," I said softly.

"Yes, honey."

"Love you."

He nodded. "Me, too."

"Dad."

"Yes."

"We'll find Mom's angel tomorrow," I said, closing my eyes.

"Pleasant dreams," he said, quietly closing the door.

As I drifted off to sleep, one star shone more brightly than the others sending a ray of light into the room. I sensed my mother kissing my forehead. I smelled her perfume. Then I had this strange dream.

It is nighttime. I am alone, looking down a dark street that is unfamiliar to me. A mist of light appears over my head, growing brighter, lighting up the street.

A woman looking neither young nor old comes floating from the light. Her light brown hair, braided with sprigs of holly, flows out behind her. She wears a shimmering white dress and in her right hand she carries a candle.

"Who are you?" I ask. As she gazes at me, her eyes are so blue and full of such light that I couldn't move.

She does not answer, turning away from me to gaze at the garbage and debris littering the Tenderloin street. From out of the night, voices of children call to me. Teens to toddlers dressed in ragged clothes rush from the run-down houses. Swarming around me, several take my hands, pulling at me, leading me through the street. They show me the poor and homeless who cower in doorways, crunched next to each other.

They reach out to me, their voices pleading. "Save the children."

"I won't look, I won't." My voice was muffled for I had bent my head, not wanting to look at them.

"Melody," they spoke louder. "Save the children."

"I can't."

"Yes, you can!"

Very slowly my head came up and I looked into her face. "I can't," I said again.

She took a long, hard look at me, and shook her head. "You'll see," she said. Then as she spoke, the street vanished and suddenly we were standing in the center of the universe. "Look!" she said, pointing her finger to the world. "Listen to the cries of the children of the poor."

"Why are you showing me all this? It's not my fault."

Her voice rang through the universe. "The rest is up to you. Find the truth."

"I don't understand you."

"You will know." Suddenly I am falling. All I can see is darkness. I am aware of shadows surrounding me, reaching out and touching me.

Then I find myself walking on a road. As I look around, I see someone walking towards me. As he comes closer, I notice it is a boy of my own age with tousled dark hair, dressed in a leather jacket and jeans.

When he sees me he frowns and walks past me. I follow him, telling him of my dream. He glances at me. "This isn't a dream," he says. Then he is gone.

I awoke to the sound of my alarm ringing. I lay there for several minutes, listening to the wind banging against my window. I was affected by the dream. I never had a dream like it before. What did it mean?

2

A Shopping Experience

My thoughts were interrupted by the loud ticking of the clock. Glancing at it, I remembered. Lelani!

I jumped out of bed. I had less than twenty minutes to meet her at the bus stop. I ran to the bathroom, quickly washed my face, and brushed my teeth.

That girl always gets in a tizzy when I'm late. I frowned a little. She should appreciate that I'm going with her at all. No one else could put up with her crazy shopping.

I looked at my reflection in the mirror. I was the sort of girl most people look twice at. Not pretty, but a pleasant face. I ran a brush through my short red hair. My amber eyes looked back at me, eyes like my mother's.

I threw on a pair of jeans and a sweater. Pulled on my boots, yanked my sloppy brown hat over my ears. Grabbed my yellow jacket, red scarf, and bounded down the stairs.

"Where are you going?" asked Mrs. Connors as I ran out the front door. I didn't answer. "Be home by six," she yelled, as I ran down the street.

I ran even faster as I turned the corner, and saw the bus coming down the hill. Lelani was jumping up and down, waving her arms and yelling at me to hurry.

I was going to make it. I got to the bus stop breathless, just as the bus came to a stop.

"Amazing," Lelani said. "You made it."

"I said I would."

"Well, you know," she said, following me on the bus, "you didn't really want to come."

"You got that right," I said, flopping in a seat next to the window.

"Melody, we'll have fun. You'll see," she said, smiling at me.

"Terrific."

As I looked out the window, I was silent. I couldn't get the dream out of my mind. It was just too scary and weird. I had never had a dream like it before.

"Anything going on with you?" Lelani asked.

I glanced at her. She had it again, that expression I knew so well. The look of concern. I thought for a moment of telling her about my dream. But I knew she would probably dismiss it, telling me it meant nothing. She didn't pay much attention to that sort of thing.

I smiled. "Not a thing."

"You seem a million miles away."

I rolled my eyes. "Hey, I'm thinking of all that fun we're going to have."

"We will, promise," she said, not too convincingly.

"Yeah, sure," I said, looking away, as the voice of a little boy grabbed my attention.

"Mommy, I want some candy."

"I told you, I don't have any candy."

Just then he peered over the top of his seat. His blue eyes were both mischievous and shy as he tried to decide whether we were friendly or not.

I smiled at him.

"Do you have any candy?"

I shook my head. "No, sorry."

He stared at me for a long moment, glanced at Lelani, then he stuck out his tongue and vanished.

"Cute kid," Lelani muttered.

After a moment, he appeared again, peering at us from around the edge of his seat.

I smiled at him again.

His face lit up. His smile grew so wide, it seemed as though his small face would break.

His mother turned to look at us. She was no more than six-

teen, with curly blond hair and eyes like her son.

"Chance, leave the girls alone," she said.

"It's okay," I said, smiling at her.

She smiled back at me. "He likes people," she said, ruffling his hair.

"Oh, really," said Lelani, bored.

"My son has so much energy," exclaimed his mother, "He wears me out sometimes!"

"Interesting," said Lelani, in that dry voice she used when she wasn't interested at all.

I shot her a look.

The boy's mother moved her hand to her curls and confided in us.

"We're staying at a homeless shelter," she said, "until we can get our own place."

I felt so sorry for her. I hesitated for a moment, then asked, "Don't you have any family you can stay with?"

She shook her head. "They don't want us, and we don't want them."

"Look," I said quickly, "I didn't mean to pry."

"You didn't," she said. "It's okay."

Chance reached up to pat his mother's cheek, as though to comfort her. "It's not too bad staying at the shelter," she said. "Chance has lots of kids to play with."

"Can't you find a job?" Lelani asked dryly.

She shrugged and glanced at her. "I've been trying really hard to find something, but I don't have a lot of job experience, which makes it tough and being homeless doesn't help."

I couldn't believe it. "You're saying no one will hire you because you're homeless?"

She nodded. "Some people feel homeless people aren't dependable. They don't want to take a chance."

"I can understand that," said Lelani.

"That's not right," I said, glaring at Lelani.

She laughed. "The way some people look at me when I tell them I'm homeless, it's like I have three heads."

"You're kidding," I said.

She shook her head. "I don't care about myself. It's my boy I worry about."

"I'm sure everything will work out for you," I said.

She smiled at me and glanced out the window. "We get off at the next stop."

As Chance scrambled from his seat, she tied his scarf around his neck, and pulled his cap down around his ears.

Reaching in my pocket, I had the urge to help her. I took out the two twenty-dollar bills my grandmother had given me for Christmas. Without the girl seeing me, I put the bills in her pocket.

Turning to us, she smiled and said, "It was nice talking to you. Have a Merry Christmas."

"You, too," I said.

Lelani looked at her. "Good luck," she said, as though she were thinking, you'll need it.

Chance suddenly turned, twisting his head sideways, grinned and winked at us.

Lelani and I couldn't help it. We burst out laughing.

"Merry Christmas, Merry Christmas," he said loudly, as his mother pushed him to the front of the bus.

"Merry Christmas," echoed many of the passengers, including the bus driver, back to the little boy who made them smile and laugh.

Through the window, I watched them cross the street. Chance turned to look at me and waved. I waved back.

"The holidays are really hard for some people," I said as I watched his mother bend down and kiss him.

Lelani nodded, looking at me thoughtfully. "Real hard," she said. She paused. "I saw what you did."

"What do you mean?" I asked, looking at her with wide-eyed innocence.

"You know exactly what I mean," she said. "Putting money in her pocket."

I shrugged. "It's no big deal. They need it more than I do."

She shook her head. "Not to worry," she said, giggling as she held up her gold credit card, "We have this."

"Girl, you are so weird," I said, laughing.

The day was chilly and gloomy, with the wind building up. Lelani and I walked slowly down the street, arms around each other. Giggling, looking in all the store windows, checking out

the Christmas displays and decorations.

I tried not to notice, but my eyes were drawn to the homeless people, sleeping in doorways, panhandling or mingling with each other. Christmas must be awful, I thought, for people who have nothing. I pushed the thought aside. It's that dream, I thought. It's not my fault they're homeless. I am not going to worry about them.

I glanced at Lelani admiring herself in the reflection of a store window. She was fair-skinned, with long shiny black hair and eyes, showing genetic kinship to her Korean mother. She was wearing a red jacket with a white hat and a white scarf tied loosely around her neck. The mix suited her. Looking away from her, I couldn't help but notice the homeless woman slowly pushing her shopping cart with all her worldly belongings down the street. A thin crooked wisp of a very old woman, she was hardly five feet tall. Her tattered gray coat hung loosely from her shoulders. She wore a brown knit cap pulled tightly over her ears. Wisps of straggly gray hair peeped out from under her cap. Leaves, holly and jingling Christmas bells bobbed on her cap as she pushed her cart.

As she came close to us, she stopped and did a strange thing. Peering through her cracked spectacles, she cocked her head and studied us thoughtfully. Her gray eyes lingered on my red hair.. She nodded her head up and down several times, looking amused.

She smiled and for a second, we locked eyes. I had this peculiar feeling that she was someone I knew. Her face was as familiar to me as if I had known her all my life. Her eyes moved from me to Lelani. I waited for her to speak - to say something. Finally she said, her voice soft and melodic, "Merry Christmas."

"Yeah," Lelani replied.

I didn't answer, only smiled. Looking into her eyes, I felt she knew why I could never celebrate Christmas again. But how could she?

She looked at us very thoughtfully for a long moment. Then she walked away a bit and turned to look at us. Her frail arm clutched her coat to her body. She walked a little more, turned to look at us again with a slight curiosity and went on down the street.

"That's one weird lady," said Lelani trying to catch a glimpse of her but she disappeared in the crowd as though the street had swallowed her.

"It must be hard for her living in the streets," I said.

Lelani shrugged. "Forget her, she's not your problem."

"You're right," I said nodding, thinking again about my dream. The more I thought about it, the less I could figure it out.

She nodded. "Like I said, it's not your problem. We're only kids, we can't change the world. Adults have to do that."

As we got closer to Macy's, she grabbed my arm. Then we began running up the street. Halfway down the block, I saw a boy sitting against the corner of a building facing us. When we got closer, I saw he was dressed too lightly for the winter weather. He looked cold as he hunched his shoulder under a leather jacket that was a little too small for him. He held a sign that read

"Hungry. Please Help."

He glanced at me - his dark eyes made him look older than his years. As we walked past him, I glanced backwards and saw he was still staring at us.

Not even trying to hide her eagerness, Lelani shoved me into the store. "If we don't hurry," she said, "All the good stuff will be gone."

Once inside Macy's, I gasped and almost turned to run back home. People of all ages and sizes were pushing and pulling merchandise off the racks. This was a real war. Personally, the very last place I wanted to be at that moment was in this store with Lelani.

I glanced at her. "Aren't those the sweaters you're looking for?" I asked, pointing to the rack.

Her eyes glazed over and without answering, she pushed through the crowd, grabbing sweaters off the racks. "I'll meet you back here later," I said. She didn't answer. I chuckled to myself as I watched a teenaged girl try her best to wrestle a sweater from Lelani. She didn't have a chance.

Doing my best to stay away from the crowds, I wandered around the store. I finally decided on a blue wool sweater for Dad, and a pair of leather gloves for Mrs. Connors.

I'll get them later, I thought. Lelani had the credit card. And knowing her as I did, she would be shopping for quite some time.

Hearing a crowd of angry voices, I wandered over to where a line of disappointed children were standing in front of an empty chair. Santa's chair. A little girl was pulling on her mother's coat, wailing, "Mommy, you said Santa was going to be here. I want to see Santa."

A little boy was pounding the floor, screaming. "You promised Santa would be here!"

All the parents were obviously tired and irritated. "Where is Santa Claus?" a father asked angrily, as his daughter kicked him in the shins.

As the crowd got noisier, a red-faced manager came out of his office. He held up his hands, trying to calm the crowd. "If you will please be quiet," he said," I will explain to you why Santa is not here."

"Let him talk," I shouted at the top of my lungs.

"Yeah, shut up," said another woman.

The crowd fell silent. "This had better be good," said the father of the boy having the temper tantrum. "I've been waiting here for two hours."

"Someone has been sending letters and telegrams, threatening Santa Claus' life," said the manager. "For his own protection, we thought it best to keep him away from the store."

"Why didn't you tell us that before," yelled an angry parent, "instead of having us wait in this line?"

"I apologize," said the manager, "for any inconvenience this may have caused you. But your children can still see Santa at the police station and the fire department, where he is under their protection."

"Now you tell us," grumbled a mother pulling her child toward the front door.

"I just can't believe it," said a woman leaving the store. "Someone threatening to kill Santa Claus. What is this world coming to?"

To the relief of the store manager, the parents quickly left with their children. "I never thought I would see the day," he told a clerk, "when I would be protecting Santa Claus."

The manager looked down as he felt someone tugging at his trousers. A little girl was staring up at him with a real mean look on her small face. When the manager smiled at her, she kicked him hard in the shins. "You made Santa go away," she said.

The embarrassed father shook his head. "We're still going to see Santa," he said. He looked at the manager and shrugged. "Kids will be kids."

The manager nodded and hobbled away painfully to his office, muttering, "Kids. I hate kids."

I wandered back to get the items I wanted. I was glad there was no crowd.

"Well, I better go find Lelani," I thought.

When I found her, I burst out laughing. She looked so comical, balancing seven different hats of all colors and shapes on her head, and carrying a huge pile of clothes.

I shook my head. Now I'd seen everything.

"Did you get everything you wanted?" I asked, walking up behind her.

She turned and peeped at me over the top of the clothes. "Not really," she whined. "All the good stuff is gone."

"You could have fooled me," I said, laughing again.

I grabbed a pile of clothes from her, took a couple of hats off her head, and carried them to the counter.

"Lelani, you won't believe this. Someone wants to kill Santa Claus!"

She turned to look at me. "He's just a fat old man in a red suit. Who needs him anyway?"

"The kids do."

She chose to ignore what I said and asked instead, "Did you find anything you wanted?"

I nodded, separating the sweater and gloves from her things. "I got these. Is it okay?"

She nodded and handed the cashier her credit card.

"I'll take my things with me," I said.

"Deliver the rest," she told the cashier.

When everything was rung up, Lelani said, "All that shopping has made me hungry. Let's go to McDonald's."

"What are you going to do with all those things you bought?" I asked as we left the store.

She glanced at me. "What do you mean?" she said. "I'm going to wear them, of course."

I shook my head. "I don't think so. I'm sure most of them will live out their lives on your closet floor."

She stared at me. "You know that's not true," she said, flipping her dark hair over her shoulder. "You know how important it is for me to look perfect. Appearance is very important."

"Lelani," I said. "There are more important things than looking perfect."

Looking me over with a critical eye, she sniffed. "It wouldn't hurt you to pay a little more attention to your appearance."

I shrugged. "I like the way I look just fine."

She sighed. "Whatever."

"Lelani," I said.

"Yeah."

I hesitated for a moment. "Well, you know, you have more clothes than anyone I know," I pointed out. "Like clothes you never wear. Why don't you give some of them away to someone who would really appreciate them."

She gave me a blank stare. "Like, to who?"

"Well, the homeless," I said. "I know they could use them."

She snorted. "Are you crazy?" she said in a strangled voice. "Give my clothes to those people? They would ruin them."

I rolled my eyes. "Girl, you're hopeless."

3

This Boy Needs Help

I saw the boy again, sitting in front of Macy's rubbing his hands and hugging himself to keep warm. As we passed by him, he spoke. "Got any spare change?"

I stopped and searched my pockets. "Sorry," I said. He nodded and smiled at me.

"Looks like it's going to rain," said Lelani, looking up at the sky. "Let's hurry. I don't want to get wet."

We had gone a half-block when I turned to look back at him. He's cold, I thought, and probably hungry, too.

"Lelani," I said sweetly, putting my arm around her.

She narrowed her eyes. "What?"

"Do you see that boy sitting in front of Macy's?"

She followed my glance. "I see him. So?"

"Let's take him to McDonald's with us."

She stared at me. "Melody, we don't know him."

"Have a heart. It's Christmas Eve and he looks hungry."

She put her hand on her hip. "I suppose if I don't say yes, you'll be mad at me."

"Hey, didn't I go shopping with you?" I reminded her.

"So you did, and you're not going to let me forget it."

I smiled at her. "Come on, Lelani."

A tiny frown tugged at her face. "Obviously, since you have no money," she said, "I will get stuck paying for his food."

"I'll pay you back, Lelani, you know I will." I stood first on one foot then the other, as she stared thoughtfully at me, trying to make up her mind. Then it began to rain.

"Well, hurry up," she snapped irritably, "And get him. I don't want to stand here and get drenched."

"Thanks, Lelani," I said. "You're the best."

"Just hurry up," she said.

I ran back to where he was still sitting, in spite of the downpour.

"My friend and I are going to McDonald's. Want to come?"

He thought for a moment. "I dunno."

"Look," I said, "in case you haven't noticed, it's raining. This is your last chance. I'm not going to ask you again."

He cocked his head, the raindrops falling in his face. "Well then, how can I refuse?"

As we ran back to where Lelani was waiting, I asked, "What's your name?"

He looked at me. "What's it to you?"

"You're getting a free meal," I said. "Don't you think I should know your name?"

"Jesse. Who're you?"

"Melody."

He grinned. "Hi."

"Lelani, this is Jesse."

As her eyes fell on Jesse, she looked down her nose at him.

"Let's go," she said, walking away quickly.

He regarded her quizzically. "Your friend doesn't like me."

"Don't mind her." I said. "She's a snob, but she'll chill out."

Inside McDonald's, long lines of people were waiting at the counter. It seemed like everyone came inside to get out of the rain.

"This is too much," grumbled Lelani. "I hate waiting."

"Try going shopping with her," I whispered to Jesse. "Talk about stress."

"What are you saying?" she asked, narrowing her eyes. By the dark look on her face, I knew she was upset because the line was moving too slowly. If I said one word she didn't like, she would use it as an excuse not to buy Jesse lunch.

I was curious about him. I wanted to know more about him.

I smiled at her. "I didn't say anything."

"Hmmph," she said, eyeing me.

Jesse glanced around and saw some friends of his sitting at a table. They waved to him. "I'll be right back," he said.

"What do you want?" I asked.

"A Big Mac and fries."

"I don't like him," said Lelani, watching him walk away.

"Oh, come on," I said, "You don't know him."

She flipped her hair. "I don't want to know him. He's so -"

"Out of your league," I interrupted her. "Is that what you're trying to say?"

"I have nothing against poor people," she sniffed. "My parents give money to help them."

"How nice," I said coldly.

Finally, we were at the counter. While we waited for our order, a couple of Jesse's friends turned to look at us, and they seemed to be laughing. Lelani glared at them. "Do you see what he's doing? He's making fun of us."

"Don't be paranoid," I said.

"He's a creep," she said angrily. "I don't know how I let you talk me into this."

As she turned away from the counter, a homeless man begging for food bumped into her, knocking her off-balance. The tray went flying and our food and drinks landed on the floor.

She turned to him, her face reddening, her eyes sparking. "You clumsy old man," she snapped. "Look what you've done!"

"Di-di-didn't mean to Miss," he stuttered nervously as he bent down to pick up the food.

Her voice rose so loud every eye in the restaurant turned to stare. "You people make me sick, always looking for a handout."

"Chill out, Lelani," I said. "You're making a fool of yourself."

Her mouth grew thin and tight. "I don't care."

The homeless man looked tired and haggard. "I-I don't want no trouble," he stuttered again." Then he turned away from her and hurried towards the door. I was so mad at her I was ready to suggest we go home, but before I could say anything, Jesse came running over.

"Hey, what's going on?" he asked.

I turned to glare at Lelani. "Ask her."

I picked up the wrapped Big Macs that still lay on the floor then followed the homeless man as he ran out the door.

"Are you okay?" I asked.

Turning his head, he didn't reply immediately. He looked into my face and nodded. "Yes."

"I wanted to tell you how sorry I am," I said handing him the sandwiches. "My friend gets weird sometimes."

His face softened and he smiled. "I understand."

I nodded. "I wish I did."

I watched him as he slowly walked down the street then disappeared around a corner. Inside the restaurant, Lelani was at it again arguing with Jesse as he tried to take the tray from her.

"I said I don't need your help."

"Oh great," I thought. "I don't need this."

As I walked up beside him, Jesse turned to look at me help-

lessly. "The manager replaced your order and she won't let me carry the tray."

"Why bother?" I said. "She wouldn't appreciate it anyway."

He glanced at Lelani who was scowling at him. "You know what?" he said. "You're right."

They made their way to a table. As Lelani put the tray down, she glared at Jesse. "Are you sure you want to be seen with us?"

He looked puzzled, then a light came over his face. "Oh, you think me and my friends were laughing at you."

She stuck a french fry in her mouth. "Well, weren't you?"

He shook his head. "Honest, we weren't," he said sincerely. "My friends always tease me when I'm with pretty girls."

"Oh, really," she said, flipping her hair over her shoulder. She quietly observed Jesse's friends who were talking and laughing amongst themselves. "Are they homeless like you?" she asked.

Jesse took a big bite out of his Big Mac. He stared at her for a moment. "Who said I'm homeless?" he asked.

She stared at him. "Duh, I never would have guessed. Your clothes, for one. And you were begging for money."

She was beginning to bore me. I made a face at her. "Come on Lelani," I said. "Give it a rest."

He was silent for a moment, studying her with his dark eyes. "Yeah, I'm homeless. Does it matter?"

"No," I said quickly, giving her a hard kick under the table.

She glared at me. "Ouch."

I met his eyes as Lelani questioned him, "Where are your parents? Why are you homeless?"

He regarded her with amusement. "You ask a lot of questions."

I shrugged. "Not that she really cares."

She stared at him. "I've never talked to anyone homeless before."

"Is that so?" he said.

"What about this morning?" I reminded her. "The girl on the bus."

She glanced at me. "He's more interesting. And besides, I wasn't talking to her, you were."

"Excuse me," I said.

He leaned across the table and leered at her. "Do I scare you?"

She puckered up her face. "No way."

"Good," he said. "I don't like scaring kids."

"You're not much older than us," I said.

"We live much different lives," he replied. "I've seen more than you ever will."

"What's it like being homeless," I asked. "Isn't it scary?"

He narrowed his eyes. "I can take care of myself. I do what I gotta do."

"I guess you have to," I said thoughtfully.

Lelani stared at him with belligerent eyes. "You really think you're tough," she said.

He grinned. "Yeah!"

I shot her a look. "How old are you, Jesse?" I asked.

He leaned back in his chair. "Old enough."

"Don't you have parents?" Lelani asked again.

He shook his head. "Ain't got no parents. I never knew my Dad, and my mother died when I was four."

"My mother's dead, too," I said.

Our eyes met. "That's tough," he said.

"Who took care of you?" I asked.

He shrugged. "Took care of myself. After my Mom died, I lived with my drunken aunt until the booze killed her. Then I hit the streets, met up with some friends and hitchhiked to San Francisco."

"Where are you from?" Lelani asked.

"Seattle."

"You have no family," I said.

He hesitated for a moment. "I have a sister somewhere."

"What happened to her?" I asked.

He was silent for a moment. "She got sick of my aunt beating up on her so she just split one night."

"How long has it been since you've seen her?" I asked

He shrugged. "I guess it's maybe three years."

Lelani looked at him. "Have you heard from her?" she asked.

He shook his head. "She left me a note saying that she'd come back for me, but she never did."

"How can she find you?" Lelani pointed out. "You're not in Seattle anymore."

"I have a friend there that I keep in touch with. If she wanted to find me, she could."

"Maybe something happened to her, Jesse," I said.

He wouldn't admit that he worried about her sometimes. "Yeah, well, she doesn't care about me, and I don't need her anyway."

"Do you stay with those kids?" I asked, looking at his friends.

He nodded. "They're my family. We don't need anyone else."

"Where do you live?" Lelani asked curiously.

"We had this really cool place under the freeway, sort of like a camp but the cops came, tore everything down, and made us move."

"Where do you live now?" she asked.

"Lots of places," he said. "Mostly in the street. When things cool down, we'll go back to the freeway."

I looked at him reflectively. "You sure have an interesting life."

"Distressing," Lelani said.

He grinned. "It's not so bad."

"When my Mom died, I felt like running away," I said. "I couldn't bear to be in the same house without her."

He stared at me. His voice was sharp. "Being homeless isn't the greatest thing that can happen to you," he said. "You get cold, tired and hungry. The cops are always bugging you. Or there could be ... worse things."

"You said it wasn't so bad," Lelani said.

Jesse's eyes fell on her. "For me," he said. "But not for you."

"Well, anyway, I don't want to live in the streets," she said flatly.

He shook his head. "I'm sure you don't," he laughed, sizing her up.

After a few seconds I said, "Things still aren't the greatest at home but I don't feel like running away anymore. My dad still rarely listens to me." I paused. "But last night, we had this conversation about angels."

Jesse and Lelani exchanged glances. "Angels?" Lelani asked.

I nodded. "Since Mom died, I've been thinking a lot about it. She always said angels watched over everyone. Like, I want to believe it's true but it's hard because I've never seen one."

Jesse listened quietly and nodded. "You don't always have to see something to know it's real."

I smiled at him. "My Mom always said that."

"I've always felt someone was watching over me," he said. "Things have happened to me that are weird."

"Like what?" I asked.

He glanced over at the table where his friends were still sitting. He looked thoughtfully at them for a moment, then looked back at us. "My friend and I were driving down this road that was so dark, we could hardly see anything. Suddenly, I heard this voice say 'Stop the car.'"

"I looked out the window. There was no one there. I looked at my friend. He didn't seem to hear anything. And it wasn't his voice I heard. Then I heard the voice again. This time, louder and more demanding. "I said stop the car!"

Jesse paused for a moment, studying our faces. Then he began again. "I knew it wasn't my imagination. I told my friend to stop the car, which was a good thing. If he hadn't we would have gone right over a cliff."

"You mean that really happened," I said.

"Yeah, it sure did."

Lelani joined in the conversation. "I think maybe there are angels. When I was little, something happened."

Jesse and I exchanged glances. "What?" I asked.

She was thoughtful. "I was about six, I think, and I was sick with this high fever. I saw a beautiful lady come into my room. She was dressed in white and glowed all over."

She paused, then continued, looking at both of us intently. "For several moments she stood staring at me. Then she took my hand and told me not to be frightened, that I would be better soon. That night the fever broke."

"Maybe you were dreaming," I said.

She shook her head. "I don't think so. It was too real. After she left, I could smell roses in my room for days but there were no roses in that room."

"Interesting," I said.

Jesse looked at me. "Do you think maybe you believe in angels now?"

I smiled at him. "Well, I admit it gives me something to think about." I looked at both of them. "I've never experienced what you have but last night I had this really strange dream."

They listened with interest until I finished. Lelani's reaction half surprised me. I never would have thought she believed in angels or dreams but you never can tell.

"That's quite a dream," she admitted.

"Well, what do you think it means?" I asked.

"Well," Jesse said, "dreams are personal."

I studied his face, thinking how much he looked like the boy in my dream, the one on the road.

"There's lots of publicity about the homeless this time of year," said Lelani. "I think maybe you're just sensitive to it."

I shook my head. "I don't think so. I've always known there were homeless people. But I never really paid much attention to them. Not like my mom did. She was always helping the poor and suffering."

Jesse smiled. "Maybe your mom is sending you a message to be more like she was."

I smiled at him. "Maybe."

"I know you won't believe me," Lelani said, "But I don't like to see people living in the street."

"You could have fooled me," I said.

She looked from Jesse to me. "You're probably thinking of that homeless man I got upset with. I shouldn't have yelled at him like I did."

"You were really mean to him," I said.

"I know, I lost my temper."

"You got that right."

I've seen him around a few times," said Jesse. "They say on the street he lost it when he saw his wife and kids burn up in a fire."

"How awful," I said.

He looked at Lelani thoughtfully. "There's lots of reasons why people are homeless and it isn't always because they want to be."

She shifted uncomfortably in her seat, showing a lack of interest.

"It's not my problem."

"Are you sure?" I asked.

Jesse studied her face. "If I see him again, I'll tell him you said you're sorry."

She shrugged indifferently.

"Why don't people do more to help the homeless?" I asked him.

His eyes darkened, and I could sense his anger. "Why should they care about the homeless? They think we're losers."

I stared at him for a moment, understanding his reaction. "Not everyone feels that way, Jesse."

"Yeah," he said. "But there's plenty that do."

"Well, " said Lelani flippantly. "There's nothing we can do about it."

"I think there is," I said.

Jesse smiled at me. "Hey, Melody! Before I forget, thank you for buying me lunch."

"Excuse me," said Lelani, "It was me who paid for your lunch."

He grinned at her. "Well, see, Lelani," he said, "you fed a poor homeless boy. You made a difference."

As the afternoon passed, Jesse and Lelani got more relaxed with each other. His friends came over to the table and hung out with us for awhile. Listening to them talk, I thought they wanted us to believe they're okay with being homeless but I could sense the uncertainty and fear they were trying to hide. I knew everyday they were living their own nightmare.

Eyeing Lelani, I saw she definitely wasn't as at ease with them as I was. Well, anyway, she wasn't screwing up her nose distastefully. Could there be hope for her after all?

After they left, we stayed in McDonald's, and talked for a long time, talking about each other's dreams and ambitions. "I've always wanted to be a fashion designer," Lelani said. "I want to make a statement."

"She'll do it, too," I said. "She always knows what she wants."

He looked at her, his eyes smiling. "You always know what you want."

She nodded. "Yeah, I do."

"What about you, Jesse?" I asked. "Don't you have any dreams?"

He got serious. "I got dreams," he said. He paused. "I want to make films that inspire people."

Lelani and I looked at him in surprise.

"You want to be a film maker?" she asked.

He nodded. "Yeah, I got this video camera someone gave me," he said. "It's like I see things with this camera that won't go away, that get inside me."

"You have a vision, Jesse," I said. "Don't lose it."

Lelani nodded. "Yeah, go for it."

He looked at me thoughtfully. "What about you? Do you have any dreams?"

I shook my head. "I want to be a journalist like my mom was. She was the best."

He watched me closely as I spoke, his eyes looking unnaturally deep. "You miss her," he said.

I nodded. "A lot."

At that moment, we both felt each other's sadness, the kind that comes when you lose someone you love. There was more - a deep understanding of the pain that follows.

"It's not wrong to hurt inside," he said.

"If you can bear it," I replied.

"It will get easier in time."

I smiled. "I'll figure out my life someday."

He nodded. "Maybe you already have."

Lelani glanced at her watch. "We have to hurry if we're going to be home by six."

He grinned as Lelani rolled her eyes. "I have absolutely no life. I'm thirteen years old, and my parents still treat me as though I'm a baby."

I nodded. "The same here. I do wish my Dad would trust me more."

"No one tells me what to do," said Jesse. "I do whatever I want and stay out as late as I want."

"You are so lucky!" Lelani and I exclaimed in unison.

He laughed. "Come on, I'll walk you to the bus stop."

When we went outside, it had stopped raining, but the wind was getting stronger. I put my hand on my head to keep my hat from blowing away. "Can you believe this wind?" I said.

"It's really weird," said Lelani.

We waited a couple of moments for the bus. When it came to a stop in front of us, I looked at Jesse and smiled. "Well, we'll see you again," I said.

He shrugged. "Yeah, well you can find me at the same place every day, unless the cops make me move."

"No problem," said Lelani. "We'll find you."

He nodded. His eyes lingered for a moment. "See you," he said before he walked away.

"See you," we said.

Looking out the window, keeping her eyes on him, Lelani remarked, "He's not so tough, he's just mad because of his life."

"Wouldn't you be," I asked, "if no one cared about you and you had to live in the street?"

She turned and looked at me. Nodding, she said, "I guess I would."

"There's lots of homeless kids like him and his friends," I said. "They deserve a better life."

Lelani turned back to the window, watching him turn the corner. "Maybe he'll find his sister," she said.

"Maybe."

When the bus came to my stop, I smiled at her. "I never thought I would be saying this," I said," but I'm glad you talked me into coming with you today."

She smiled. "Me, too."

"Call me," I said, leaving the bus.

"I will."

4

Who is Thelma?

Walking the three blocks home from the bus stop, emotions were welling up inside me as I thought about Jesse, the homeless girl and her son. Why do people have to live in the street? It just doesn't seem right. Suddenly, I heard the sound of footsteps behind me. I looked around, staring down the street. No one was there. I walked a little faster, I heard them again. I stopped, they stopped. "All right," I said, stopping and looking around again, "Where are you?"

There was silence. Then from out of nowhere I saw her; pushing her shopping cart past me. Her eyes were looking down, seeing only her feet. Without looking my way, I knew she had seen me. Then she stopped for a moment and looked back at me. Her voice broke the silence. "You, girl, come here."

Curiously, I walked to her.

"Why are you staring at me?" she asked.

"I'm not."

"Yes you are. What's so fascinating about me anyway?"

I admit I was staring. I couldn't mistake those jingling Christmas bells, or those cracked spectacles. I met her gaze without flinching. "Hey, you're that woman I saw downtown today."

Her eyes twinkled and she chuckled, "Am I, now?" She looked me over from head to toe. "Take off your hat," she demanded, "so I can get a look at you."

I was kinda' amused at her fascination with my hair. I took off my hat and she chuckled again, nodding several times. "Your hair sure is red."

I looked at her quizzically. Then I held out my hand. "My name is Melody."

She stiffened a little and scratched her head. Then she took my hand. "Thelma is my name."

I smiled. "Hi, Thelma."

The old woman threw me a glance without responding. Then she looked up at the sky, nodding. "Storm coming in," she said. "Big one, too."

"Where did you come from, Thelma?" I asked, staring at her.

She looked back at me, her eyes crinkling, a tiny smile on her face. Then she put her finger to her lips and whispered. "Out of nowhere."

Looking at her I felt affection for her mixed with pity, as I glanced at the worn gloves and tattered clothes she was wearing. "Here," I said, handing her the bag from Macy's. "These will keep you warm."

Keeping her eyes on me, she took the bag and opened it. Seeing the sweater and gloves, she nodded and smiled at me. Then, she closed the bag, placing it in her cart, underneath some blankets and old clothes.

She looked at me very thoughtfully. "Thank you," she said.

I nodded, smiling at her.

Her smile broadened. "Merry Christmas."

I suddenly had a thought. "Come on, Thelma," I said.

"Where to?" she asked.

"Are you hungry?"

"I could eat a little."

"My house is just down the street. I'll get you something to eat."

"That's nice."

Walking along, I saw her glance at me several times with a tiny smile on her wrinkled face. I was puzzled by her. She could be anyone's grandmother. Why was she living in the street?

"Thelma," I asked, "why are you in this neighborhood?"

She stopped, then leaned forward and raised her index finger to my face. "I have some important business to take care of," she said quietly.

"You know someone who lives around here?" I asked.

A smile crossed her wrinkled lips. "Maybe I do."

"Maybe I know them, too," I said.

Her laughter was a ripple of silver. "Oh, I think you do," she said, then fell silent. I listened to the steady patter of our footsteps and the rattle of her shopping cart as she pushed it. Now I heard the wind; it seemed to be whispering over and over, "You can't escape, you can't escape." What did it mean? I didn't understand. I looked at Thelma, unable to take my gaze from her face. She moved her eyes to mine and looked thoughtfully at me for a moment, then nodded silently.

When we came to my house, I hesitated. She looked so cold and frail. "Do you want to come inside?" I asked. "It's awfully cold outside."

She shook her head. "Oh no, dear, I'm fine." Then she backed her shopping cart up towards the stairs and gazed off into the distance as though she was waiting for something, or someone.

I ran up the stairs and looked back at her. "Now, don't you go away," I said. "I'll be right back." She smiled softly and pushed a wisp of hair off her brow.

"Okay," she said.

Once inside the house, I was glad no one was home. Thelma was my secret. I didn't want to share her with anyone. Anyway, the way dad was acting lately, I was sure he wouldn't approve. Nothing I did was right.

I quickly made Thelma two thick ham sandwiches, poured some hot chocolate in a thermos and cut her a large piece of cake. Returning outside, I saw her sitting on the step with her head in her lap. I got really concerned. "Thelma," I asked, "are you all right?"

She was silent, not moving. I touched her on the shoulder, and shook her gently. Her head jerked up. "Oh, it's you," she said, smiling. "Did you bring me something to eat?"

I nodded, handing her the food. Our eyes met and held. "I never met a girl like you," she said. Watching her eat, I felt sad for her. I wanted to comfort her, to do something for this poor woman that no one cared about.

"Thelma," I asked, "don't you have a family?"

"Oh yes," she said, nodding her head.

"Where are they?"

She took a bite from her sandwich, then peered at me. "Don't you know?"

"How could I?" I thought. I knew nothing about her. We stared at each other as she finished eating. Wrapping the piece of cake neatly in a napkin, she said, "I'll save this for later."

Then she lifted her head, listening to the wind, nodding several times, as though it were speaking to her. "I have to go now," she said. She grasped my arm and struggled to get up off the steps. "I can't get up!"

I grabbed both her upper arms and pulled her gently up off the steps. She smiled at me. "Thank you."

"Where will you go?" I asked.

She studied my face. "No need for you to worry about me."

I couldn't help it - I felt a little sad as I watched her wheel her shopping cart away. "Thelma," I called. "Wait a minute." She stopped and turned to look back at me.

"Mind if I walk a little way with you?" I asked humbly.

She looked into my face questioningly. "What do you know about being poor and homeless?"

"I'm trying to understand, Thelma."

She gazed at me, nodding her head up and down several times.

"Good," she said. "That's good."

All day the wind had been rising. The leaves from the trees rose toward the wind. "You go home now," she said.

As I watched her walk away, I saw a strange glow of light surrounding her. "Thelma," I called out to her. "Who are you?"

She turned and looked back at me. "Don't you know? I am your guardian angel."

From somewhere a church bell rang five times. I watched her round the corner of a building, and I followed. Then a strange thing happened. Thelma seemed to be flying rather than walking, looking neither to the right nor left, only looking up at the sky. A clap of thunder followed, as though she knocked and it answered. Then, she disappeared from sight. At that moment, all I could do was stare wide-eyed, not quite believing what I saw.

"Are you really my guardian angel?" I whispered. Another clap of thunder, followed by lightning, flashed in the sky.

5

The Music Played On

Later that night, as I lay in bed, I stared at the ceiling letting my mind drift back to the last few hours. I heard the wind getting louder, followed by more thunder and lightning. Rain spattered against the half-open window I had forgotten to close. I got up to close the window and the floor creaked as I walked across it. Looking out, I didn't see at first the figure as it approached, wearing a long hooded red cloak, which concealed the face. Then I saw him, outlined in the light of the street lamp that flickered on and off, because of the storm. I stood motionless, staring out the window. He seemed to pause as we stared at each other. Then he turned away and walked quickly into the night, dissolving into the raindrops.

I shivered with excitement, waiting for something. For what, I did not know. I turned restlessly in my bed, listening to the wind howling in. The thunder was growing closer.

I closed my eyes and opened them again. I sat straight up in bed. My heart was racing. A small figure appeared in the doorway. Although his face was not visible to me because of the darkness, there was something familiar about him. I took a deep breath and turned on the lamp by the bed. It was a young boy with curly blonde hair.

He gazed at me. "Chance," I said. "What are you doing here?"

He laughed and came to the side of the bed, pulling at me to get up. "You want me to come with you?" I said. He nodded and laughed again.

"Okay," I said, jumping out of bed. "Let's go."

He took my hand. I followed him down the hall and out the front door. Outside, the wind was howling in the trees. I tried to keep from shivering, with the rain falling heavily on me. "What's going on?" I asked him. He just smiled.

Suddenly, the rain stopped. Bells were tolling in all directions. Before my eyes, the street came to life in a blaze of Christmas lights and decorations. I couldn't move. Looking on in amazement, I saw children come from everywhere, each one wearing a crown of holly around their heads. The music began softly at first, as they took my hands, laughing, leading me away to dance with them. The music got stronger and stronger and more exciting. And the whole street was full of dancing children. We danced up and down the street and round and round the large Christmas tree that stood in the square. We danced by the figure in the red cloak who stood silently watching. "Why does he look so sad?" I thought to myself. I wanted to know his sorrow but I continued to dance.

Then I heard a familiar voice. "Melody," he said, "What's happening? How did I get here?"

I reached for his hand. "Dance with us, Jesse."

He pulled away. "This is just some weird dream. I'm going to wake up in a minute."

"I'll dance with you," said Lelani, her eyes bright with sudden excitement. She then grabbed me around the waist and began to dance.

We danced by Jesse again. "Dance with us," the children said. We danced and danced all through the streets, calling to him, until he, too, caught up in the infectious rhythm, swayed with the music. We danced all through the night. Then, just before dawn, the music stopped. The children stood still, looking up into the sky, listening to the sound of a train whistle coming closer and closer.

"Awesome!" said Jesse, staring at the train coming down from the sky.

6

A Ride On A Train

"This is not real," said Lelani, looking stunned.

The train rattled to a stop a few feet from us. The doors opened, and a conductor stepped off the train. "All aboard!" he shouted.

I looked at him. "Is this train for us?" He nodded.

"I have a feeling," said Jesse, "that this is going to be a cool trip."

As I got on the train, I looked back over my shoulder. The street was still and dark. The Christmas lights, the children, everything had vanished. "I'm sure there's a reasonable explanation for all this," Lelani said as she followed me onto the train.

Glancing around, I saw all the seats were empty except for

one. I wasn't surprised to see her. "Hi, Thelma," I said, sitting next to her. "We meet again."

She nodded, smiling. "Hello," she said.

Lelani plopped in the seat across from her. Her eyebrows came together. "I know you. You're that old woman Melody and I saw."

Thelma stared at her, frowned, then laughed heartily. "You're sure of that?"

Jesse stared at her curiously. "Hey Melody, introduce me to your friend."

"Her name is Thelma." I took a deep breath. "She's my guardian angel."

Lelani rolled her eyes. "Oh really," she said sarcastically. "I never would have guessed."

Thelma frowned at Lelani then smiled. "That's right," she said. "I am."

Lelani turned up her nose. "You don't look like an angel."

"Angels wear many different disguises," Thelma answered.

"I believe you," said Jesse.

Thelma smiled. "You're a very smart boy."

Lelani shrugged and turned away to gaze out the window. "This is ridiculous," she thought. "She can't be an angel. Who is she, anyway?"

Thelma's lips didn't move, but Lelani heard her say, "I am who I am."

"Why are we here, Thelma?" I asked.

Jesse nodded. "I was just thinking the same thing."

"Because you need to find the truth."

"Excuse me," said Lelani, turning to stare at her. "What are you talking about?"

Thelma narrowed her eyes and looked at Lelani. "You will find out soon enough."

The train made several stops, picking up other passengers - men, women, and children from slums, the streets, and poor neighborhoods. Each glanced soberly at Thelma as they sat quietly in their seats. One man played a somber tune on his harmonica. His manner was simple and his demeanor sad but honest. I could not help but feel both respect and sympathy. I wanted to know all I could about each one of them. Who were they? Why were they on the train?

"Who are these people, Thelma?" I asked softly.

I noticed now that, for the first time, her face was grave. She was silent for a moment as she steadily gazed at them. Then she spoke. "They are the spirits of the poor and homeless who have died from poverty and disease."

Jesse looked at her questioningly. "You mean they're ghosts."

Thelma nodded. "Yes," she answered slowly. "The forgotten ones."

"Kids aren't supposed to die," Lelani said.

"They do everyday," answered Thelma quietly.

"It's not fair," I said.

I could see the sadness in Jesse's face. I felt like crying. If anyone understood, he did, living in poverty every day. Thelma studied him for a long moment. "Life isn't always fair," she finally said.

Lelani shook her head and turned towards the window. "Look," she exclaimed. "We're going up into the sky!"

It was nothing like I had ever seen before. Looking out the window, it was like the sky at home but different, clearer, brighter. After a while, the doors opened into the heavens to a light so blinding we could not look into it. A joyous look came across the children's faces as they got up and left their seats. Some people carried children, others walked with them into the light.

A small boy hesitated and turned to look back at Thelma. She smiled at him and his whole face lit up with happiness. Then he shook his head and walked into the light.

"Where are they going, Thelma?" asked Lelani.

"Someplace where they won't be judged for what they are, but who they were."

Lelani thought very hard about it for a moment. "I see what's happening," she said quietly. "And I'm beginning to understand the reason".

Thelma answered her in a voice which was low but audible.

"Truth is important," she said.

We were silent for a long time, unable to put out of our minds what we had seen.

I looked at Jesse with mounting dismay. Why wasn't someone there to help him when he needed it?

"Melody, are you all right?" he asked.

I nodded. "I'm okay."

Thelma looked at me thoughtfully. I knew she understood.

7

He's An Old Friend

Suddenly, the train began shaking back and forth.

"Hey, what's happening?" Lelani asked.

"Just a little turbulence," Jesse said.

Terror gripped my heart. The train was rapidly descending, fighting a powerful wind that shook it like a rag.

"I don't like this one bit," said Lelani, clutching Jesse.

Thelma shook her head, chuckling. "You have nothing to be afraid of."

I closed my eyes as the violent storm shook the train again.

Thelma placed her hand on mine. "It's alright, Melody."

"Yes!" I said, breathing a tremendous sigh of relief when the train was safely on the ground. A moment later the doors opened.

"Well, what're you waiting for?" said Thelma. "Get going."

"What are you talking about, Thelma?" said Jesse, peering outside. "There's a bad storm out there."

"He's waiting," she said. "You must hurry."

I looked at Jesse and Thelma.

"Who's waiting?" I asked.

"Stop asking so many questions. There is not much time."

"We aren't exactly dressed to go outside. We're still wearing our nightclothes," Lelani said.

Thelma shook her head, "Look again."

Lelani and I were surprised to see we had on the same clothes we wore earlier. Around Jesse's neck was a bright red scarf that we hadn't seen before.

"Go on, now," she said.

Jesse looked out at the raging storm. "I guess there's no reasoning with you."

"Go!" she said again.

When we stepped outside we were instantly covered with snow. The storm struck us full in the face. As we trudged through the snow, the violent storm howled around us, as though it were laughing at us. "This is some bad weather," I said, wiping the snow from my face.

"If you ask me, this is ridiculous," said Lelani. "We don't even know where we're going."

Jesse allowed himself to laugh. "Yeah," he said, "or who we're supposed to see."

"I think we're going to find out," I said, pointing to a light that seemed to make a path for us.

We followed the light. As we got closer, we saw a red brick house, partially hidden by the snowstorm. A woman appeared in the doorway. She was dressed in a bright red dress and wearing a white apron. Her hair was as white as the snow. Her face shone as she smiled at us. "I'm so glad you're here," she said. "Please come inside out of the storm."

We hurried up the steps and followed her into a spacious living room that was cheerfully decorated with Christmas decorations. A festive tree stood in the corner, and a cozy fire was burning in the fireplace. "Take off your jackets and scarves," she said, "and warm yourselves in front of the fireplace. I'll be right back with some hot drinks for you."

Standing there as we warmed ourselves in front of the fireplace, Lelani was the first to notice him, sitting quietly in a leather chair. His white hair was long, falling beneath his shoulders. His beard almost reached his breast. She let out a little shriek. "It's you!" she said.

Jesse and I turned to look at him. "My gosh, it's Santa Claus!" I said.

He nodded soberly. "I'm called by many names."

I stared curiously at him. Why, he was the one I saw beneath my window, the same one who watched us dancing. Why does he look so sad?

Mrs. Claus came back into the room. She was carrying a tray.

"I brought you some hot cider," she said. "and some gingerbread cookies I just baked this morning."

I took a cookie. Biting into it, I said, "This is sure the best cookie I've ever eaten."

Lelani nodded.

Jesse was silent. He took a cup of cider and nibbled on a cookie, staring intently at Santa. Taking another bite, I asked, "Why are we here?"

Mrs. Claus set the tray on the table. "Because Santa says Christmas is dead."

I stared at him. I couldn't believe what she was saying. "What are you saying? Christmas is not dead!"

Santa stood up then. He walked to the window staring out at the storm. "There is so much hatred and violence in the world," he said sadly. "People just don't care about each other anymore."

Jesse shifted around, uneasy-like. He could understand what Santa was saying. He lived with it his whole life. "Yeah," he thought. "The whole world's messed up."

I had to make him understand. "You can't disappoint kids because of what people do."

Santa turned slowly to look at us. "What's the use? No one believes in me anymore."

Lelani shook her head. "How can you say that? Lots of children believe in you."

"I'm just a fat old man in a red suit. Who needs me anyway?"

"All right," Lelani said. "I admit I was wrong. Don't pay any attention to me. No one else does."

"I'm just a fantasy. I'm not real."

"You're the spirit of Christmas," I said. "We need you."

He shook his head. "There is no more spirit," he answered sadly. "Each year it died a little more."

" I was at Macy's today," I said. "And there were plenty of kids who were upset because you weren't there."

Santa raised his eyebrows expressing curiosity.

"Really?" he said.

I nodded. "Someone has been sending death threats to the store. They sent your helpers to the police and fire department. The children went there to see you."

"Are you telling me someone wants to kill me?"

"It's no big thing," said Lelani. "There's always weirdos out there."

"Oh, I see..." he said.

"Hey, look at it this way," I said. "If someone wants to kill you, then they must believe in you."

He nodded. "You have a point."

"Well, then go for it," Lelani said.

"I don't know."

"Except for my father, you are the most stubborn person I ever met." I shook my head. "Are you going to let all those kids down?"

Santa did not know what to say. There was a long moment of silence and Jesse said, "He's let kids down before."

This surprised him. "Have I let you down, Jesse?"

"You could say that."

Santa realized that he had to know how this tragedy came about. "Jesse, didn't you ever write me a letter?"

"Yeah, once. My drunken aunt burnt it up with a cigarette. She said you weren't real."

"I'm sorry. I never received your letter Jesse."

"Well, excuse me," Jesse said. "All my sister and I ever had to play with was empty liquor bottles."

Santa's heart was filled with sadness as he looked into Jesse's eyes and saw the hurt and pain that was there. It was always the children who suffered the cruelty of others. "I try to visit every house," he said. "But sometimes I miss a few. That's why letters are so important."

Jesse shrugged. "It don't matter no more. But you can't let those other kids down, especially the poor ones."

Santa sighed. "It's not that I don't care about the children. I do. That's why I became Santa Claus, to make toys for poor children. Then I realized it doesn't matter if a child is rich or poor. Every child is important."

"Then do what you're supposed to do," said Jesse. "Do your thing and deliver those toys."

Santa burst out laughing. "You're right, Jesse. I won't disappoint the children."

Jesse nodded. "Good," he said.

Santa looked at Mrs. Claus. "Do I have time?"

She smiled and nodded.

"Come with me," he said. "I want to show you something."

We followed him down the stairs and into a large play area. There were children everywhere, laughing and playing. "Santa's here, Santa's here!" several yelled, running up to him. The children swarmed all around him, happy to see him. He laughed, patting several children on the head.

"Play with us, Santa," they said.

He laughed again and hugged one small boy. "I'll play with you when I return home," he said. His eyes twinkled. "Tonight is Christmas Eve and I have lots of toys to deliver."

"It's about time you got some sense in you," said a boy walking up to him.

"This is Billy," Santa said to us, smiling.

Billy nodded. "His top assistant. If it wasn't for me nothing would get done around here."

"Quite so," agreed Santa. "I don't know what I'd do without him."

I stared at the children. They seemed so happy. "Are these your children?" I asked.

He shook his head. "They are abandoned and abused children I found living in the streets. I try to find good homes for them but some, like Billy, prefer to stay here."

"That's because you know you need me," said Billy.

Santa nodded to us. "He's right. I do."

Jesse looked at him. "You're alright," he said.

Santa smiled. "Thank you, Jesse," he said, "That means a lot to me coming from you."

Jesse smiled back.

"Billy, show these young people around," Santa said. "It's time I got ready for my journey."

Then Santa went back upstairs, and Billy cheerfully gave us a guided tour of the dormitories where the children slept. Wonderful, spicy smells - cinnamon, nutmeg, and cloves - filled the country style kitchen, where all the cookies were being baked. And finally, the best place of all - Santa's toy factory.

"Hey, this is alright!" exclaimed Jesse, staring at the hundreds of workers of all ages, making toys, working on the assembly lines, putting the toys neatly on shelves.

Billy looked at Jesse. "You can stay with us if you want. Santa always says there's room for a few more."

Jesse shook his head. "I gotta go. I have things to do."

I nodded. "Jesse has a lot of friends that would miss him."

"Well, if you ever change your mind," Billy said.

Jesse grinned. "I'll be back sometime."

Billy nodded. "Bring your friends. They would always be welcome here."

"I'll remember that," said Jesse.

"Let's go to the barn," said Billy. "You can see Santa take off."

It had stopped snowing. The air was still and quiet. Lelani and I paused to look at the breathtaking view. The mountains, the pines and fir trees glistened with a whiteness we had never seen before. When she spoke she did not look at me. "She really is an angel," she said.

"Yes," I answered.

She was silent for a long moment. Then she turned to me. "I didn't believe it at first but I do now."

I nodded and smiled at her.

Her eyes fell on Jesse and Billy, walking ahead of us into the barn. "Jesse needs an angel to help him," Lelani said.

"He has one," I answered. "Everyone does."

After a moment she slowly nodded. "I think you're right."

When we went into the barn Santa was harnessing his reindeer. "Are you ready, Santa?" Billy asked.

Santa chuckled. "As ready as my reindeer. Right, boys?"

The reindeer nodded several times and moved around impatiently, for they were eager to get started on their journey.

Jesse stood silently for a moment. He petted the reindeer, then glanced at Santa. "I wanted to believe in you," he said. "But I couldn't."

Santa looked at him and smiled. "It's alright, Jesse," he said gently. "I understand."

Jesse looked long and hard at him. He knew in his heart that he did.

Santa placed his hand on his shoulder. "You're going to be alright."

Jesse nodded. "I know."

Santa threw his bag of toys into the sleigh and climbed in. He looked at us with a curious expression on his face. "Is there anything you want for Christmas?" he asked.

As I thought about it, Jesse suddenly said, "There's nothing you can't do. Will you bring Melody's mother back?"

I stared at him in disbelief.

Lelani nodded. "You're Santa Claus. You can work miracles."

Santa was silent for a moment, thinking of what they asked him He sighed and shook his head. "There's some things even I can't do."

I believed him. I knew my mother couldn't come back.

"It's okay," I said. "If you could bring her back, you would."

Santa nodded his head then he looked at Jesse. "Are you sure there's nothing you want?" he asked again.

"Nah, nothing. Just don't forget those poor kids."

He looked at Lelani questioningly and she smiled. "From this Christmas on, forget my presents. Give them to the poor."

"You're sure of that?" he asked.

She smiled. "Positive."

"Me, too!" I said. As Santa looked at us wordlessly, I suddenly had a though. I whispered in his ear. He smiled and said, "I'll work on it," he said.

Lelani took a long, hard look at him.

"Don't give up on people," she said.

He smiled at her reassuringly. "I won't."

"People can change," she continued. "We have to find a way to bring everyone together to make this a better world."

He didn't say anything for a moment, but sat looking at us thoughtfully. Then he said. "You can make it happen. Each of you can."

As his reindeer flew up into the sky, I said," I never thought I would see this."

"Me neither," said Lelani as he called down to us.

"Merry Christmas! Merry Christmas!"

At that moment, we heard the sound of the train whistle blowing.

"Thelma's waiting for you," said Mrs. Claus, who had come outside.

"I'm so glad we came here," I said, smiling at her.

She smiled and hugged each of us. "I'm glad you came too."

Billy nodded. "You be sure to come back sometime."

"We will," I said.

Mrs. Claus looked into my eyes and whispered. "Believe in your dreams Melody." Then she gave us a big bag of cookies to eat on the way home.

Walking back to the train, I asked, "Do you think anyone would believe this?"

"I don't think so," said Lelani.

Jesse shook his head. "No way."

"Everything turned out alright," I said, plopping in the seat next to her again.

She peered at me over the top of her spectacles. "Never thought it wouldn't."

"Hey Thelma," said Jesse smiling at her. "That Santa Claus guy is cool."

"Definitely cool," said Thelma.

"Well," Lelani said, "this has been one interesting adventure."

Thelma looked at her thoughtfully. "How d'you mean?"

Lelani didn't say anything for a moment, but sat in her seat staring at the floor. "Well," she said, "I saw a side of me I didn't like."

"Did you now?" asked Thelma.

It surprised me when Lelani admitted, "I've been really selfish and mean."

Thelma looked at Lelani and said, "People can change."

Lelani nodded and smiled.

"You made all this happen, Thelma," I said. "But why?" I asked, my voice heavy with questions.

As I said that, Lelani and Jesse suddenly fell asleep leaning against the back of their seat.

Thelma gazed at me for a moment and then said, "If you look in your heart, you'll find the answer."

"I doubt that," I replied looking at Jesse and Lelani. I felt her watching me. "Melody," she called my name softly.

I turned back to her. "Is there something you wish?" she asked.

I thought for a moment, then asked her, "My mom, is she alright?"

"Yes."

I tried to keep the tears from showing. "Tell my mom I love her and I miss her alot."

She placed her hand gently over mine. "She knows," she said.

I heard those words and turned to the window staring out at the couds. "I want to believe you," I said in a small voice.

And Thelma answered, "Ask her yourself. She's standing right beside you."

"Mom," I said, not believing what I saw. "Is it true? Is it you?"

She smiled at me. "It's me," she said.

I stood up and put my arms around her. "But how?" I asked.

"You have a couple of good friends who can't bear to see you unhappy. It's because of them I'm here."

I was puzzled for a moment, then I understood. Jesse's and Lelani's Christmas wish was for me to see my mother. "They're the best," I said.

"I know," she answered.

"Mom, I miss you so much."

She stroked my hair. "Everything will be alright. You'll be alright."

"Not without you. I want to be with you."

She gently pulled herself away from me. "Your father loves and needs you more than ever. Take care of him. I have to go now."

"Where are you going?"

"It's a long way from here."

"Mom, please don't leave me."

And then she gazed into my eyes and said; "Listen to your heart, Melody." Suddenly everything became clear in my mind.

My mother was telling me my life had a purpose - to make people understand that only by helping others could we make this a better world. And when I looked at her and remembered how she opened her heart to those in need, I was glad.

Then she kissed me on the forehead and whispered. "I will never leave you. I will always be with you." And with one final smile she was gone.

I didn't say anything for a while then I met Thelma's gaze. We stared at each other for a long time.

"Are you alright?" she asked.

I smiled at her. "I am now," I said. Then I leaned my head against her shoulder. "After all this is over, will I ever see you again?"

And Thelma answered, "Yes, Melody, you'll be seeing me again."

8

Home Again

I awoke with the sun streaming through the window. I felt different - as if things were going my way for a change. I jumped out of bed. "Today's Christmas," I yelled.

I was just running down the stairs when the telephone rang. "I'll get it," I shouted, and picked up the receiver.

"Merry Christmas!" a voice said cheerfully.

"Hi, Lelani, Merry Christmas to you too," I said.

She paused, then said suddenly, "I've been doing a lot of thinking about what you said yesterday."

"What's that?" I asked.

She paused again. "You know, giving my clothes to the homeless."

I pulled the phone away from my ear and stared at it. There really are Christmas miracles. I put the phone back. "What brought about this change of heart?" I asked.

"Oh, I guess meeting Jesse and everything."

"Really," I said.

"Will you go with me to the homeless shelter today?" she asked.

"Sure," I said, then added, "you have lots of things you could give away."

"Girl, you're always thinking," she said, laughing.

"But of course."

"My parents are entertaining some friends that are visiting for the holidays," she said. "I'll call a taxi and pick you up."

"Don't do that. I'll ask my dad to take us."

"If you don't think he'll mind."

"I can ask."

When I told dad what Lelani wanted to do, he said, "I was going to go to the shelter today, anyway."

Then I remembered. "Mom's gifts," I said.

He nodded. "She bought them for the children at the shelter a few days before the accident."

I followed dad to the hall closet. "She had me put them on the top shelf," he said. "I almost forgot they were there."

As he reached up and took the box off the shelf, a smaller box fell to the floor. We stared at each other. "Mom's angel," I said.

He shook his head. "I can't believe it. It was here all the time."

He lifted the angel out of the box and stared at it for a long moment, then he handed it to me. We went back into the living room. Then dad lifted me on his shoulder, and I very carefully put Mom's angel on the top of the tree.

"Perfect!" he exclaimed, looking up at it.

"Perfect!" I said.

He looked thoughtfully at me, and went and sat on the couch. "Honey," he said. "Sit here. I want to talk to you."

I looked at him. "What did I do now?"

He shook his head. "Actually, I wanted to apologize to you."

I stared at him. Could this be true, dad apologizing to me? I sat next to him. "I'm sorry, I've been such a jerk," he said. "When your Mother died, I forgot for a while that I have a daughter I love very much. I'd like to make it up to you if you will let me."

"Sure, Dad," I said, hugging him. "It'll be okay."

He smiled. "I'm glad of that," he said. "I was a little worried you might not want to hang out with your old dad."

"Hey, not all the time," I responded promptly. "I need some time to be with my friends."

He nodded. "I understand."

At the homeless shelter we passed out the gifts. Afterward, Lelani helped the girls try on the clothes. I read my favorite Christmas story, Dickens' "A Christmas Carol" to the children. When I finished reading the story, a familiar little boy ran up to me. "We're going home," he said.

I smiled at him. "You are?"

The woman with him nodded. I remembered her from the bus. "Hi," I said, smiling at her.

She smiled back. "You gave me the confidence I needed to call my parents," she said. "They were searching for us everywhere. They want us to come home."

"I'm glad for you," I said sincerely.

She nodded. "We have a lot of things to work out."

"It's going to be a good Christmas for you after all," I said.

She nodded. "It's a beginning."

"Will you come and visit us?" Chance asked.

I leaned down, giving him a hug. "I can't promise," I said. "But I'll write you lots of letters."

He thought about it for a moment. Then a big grin came across his face. "Okay," he said, and then went off to play with his friends.

On the way home, I asked my dad to drive past Macy's. There he was sitting in his usual spot. Just as I was going to call to him, I saw a dark-haired woman running across the street, calling his name.

I nudged Lelani. As Jesse recognized her, he stood up. A grin came across his face as she came closer. They stood talking for a moment, then they hugged each other. "Jesse's sister," exclaimed Lelani. I nodded. "Thank you, Santa," I whispered.

It's strange but I still think about Thelma all the time. Dad said it never happened, that it was only a dream. Maybe he's right. I don't know. All I know for certain is she changed my life.

Is it true? Could Thelma have been my guardian angel? I always thought so.

It was nearly dawn when I finished writing the story.
As I left the building it began to rain. There wasn't a taxi in sight. The street was nearly deserted except for a few people and the occasional passing car.

I hurried down Sixth Street, toward Mission, looking for a taxi. I wanted to get out of this rain and get home as quickly as I could. Suddenly, through the downpour I noticed a familiar old woman come from around the corner pushing a shopping cart. "Could it be?" I thought.

I followed her for several blocks. As she came to a narrow alley, she hesitated and turned to look at me. For a moment, we stood motionless staring at each other. Then she nodded, smiled that wonderful smile of hers and walked into the alley. I stared after her, looking in all directions, but she had disappeared.

As I returned to the street, the full force of the torrential rain hit me. A taxi appeared. It moved cautiously, rhythmically through the storm. As I ran for it, it slowed to a stop in front of me.

The door swung open. "Hey, Miss Ryan. You're getting all wet," said the driver. In spite of the raincoat, I was soaked.

"George, I'm sure glad to see you," I said getting into the taxi.

"Been a long night?" he asked.

"Yes," I said.

"You going home now?"

"Yes, George. Take me home."

I rested my head against the window and as I stared out the window, trying to see through the storm, my mind began to wander. Had it really happened? Then the rain lifted and for an instant, I was in another place, lost in the memory of her eyes.

As I got out of the taxi, I asked him, "George, do you believe in angels?"

He smiled. "Yeah, I guess I do."

I smiled back at him. "Merry Christmas, George."

He nodded. "Merry Christmas, Miss Ryan."

As I walked up the steps to my front entrance, I thought, "I'll search for her tomorrow." But I knew in my heart I would never see her again."

Free Spirit

Helping to build a future for a lost generation.

The Bay Area and the rest of the United States has a visible and growing problem with homeless and at-risk youth. Experts estimate that thousands of these youth, ages 13 to 21, are on the street. Most fend for themselves and lead dangerous and unfulfilled lives.

Providing kids with the love and attention they need to turn their lives around has become Barbara's personal crusade.

Free Spirit Productions, founded by Barbara Neal in 1985, proposes to help these troubled youths by helping them to develop creative outlets. Free Spirit provides a caring, non-competitive atmosphere in which to enhance artistic expression.

Many prominent local artists and performers have volunteered their time and talents to this worthy cause. Barbara, herself, acts as a teacher, mother and counselor to dozens of teenagers from all backgrounds.

Barbara and her dedication to the kids, along with the generous support of the community are providing these inner city youth with an opportunity to succeed.

The Free Spirit Choir is the voice of the organization. Its inspirational, raw talents have met with rousing success at every performance while developing confidence and skills in its members.

Free Spirit is helping youth deal with the realities of inner city life — gangs, drugs, relationships and problems at home.

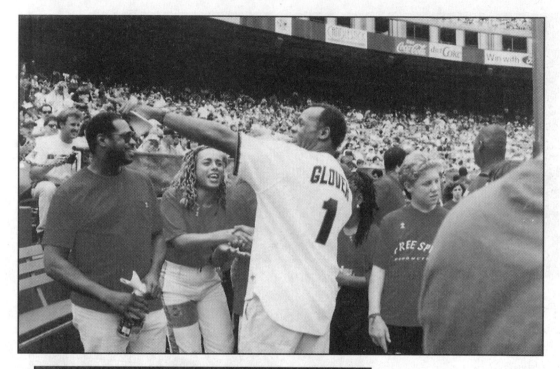

Many local
celebrities have
joined Barbara's
crusade.
Danny Glover has
become one of Free
Spirit's biggest fans
and supporters.